www.mascotbooks.com

Red Seat Media, LLC
Visit our website at www.redseatmedia.com
Follow us on Twitter at @redseatmedia

First Printing: December 2011
Second Printing: June 2013

For more information, please contact:
Mascot Books
560 Herndon Parkway #120
Herndon, VA 20170
info@mascotbooks.com

Library of Congress Control Number: 2013936642

CPSIA Code: PRT0613A
ISBN-10: 162086259X
ISBN-13: 9781620862599

Printed in the United States

Welcome to Plow Town

The Plow Family Adventures™

Story by Jamie & Chuck Freedman

Illustrated by Kory Fluckiger

Red Seat Media, LLC - Boston, MA

This book is dedicated to our sons, Chase and Isaac, and to all the children in our lives who bring happiness to our family and friends: Addison, Ben, Callie, Cameron, Chloe, Connor, Dahlia, Damani, Elijah, Ella, Emma, Emmet, Gregory, Izumi, Jacob, Jake, Jonas, Julian, Kaiya, Katie, Kyle, Kylie, Leah, Madeira, Maelyn, Maia, Noah, Sarah, Sevrin, Stella, and Victoria.

A special thanks to our friends and family for their support, ideas, and inspiration.

- Jamie and Chuck Freedman

The Plow family lives in a two-garage apartment beneath the highway. After a long and busy winter, they can finally sleep.

It is springtime and flowers are
about to bloom. Abby, the youngest
Plow, is eager to get back to work.

"Is it winter yet?" she asks her older brother.

"No," says Gregory, a red Jeep plow.
"Go back to sleep."

Months go by and it's another season.

Abby wakes her mother, Sandy, a sand truck plow. "Is it winter yet, Mom?"

"No," she replies. "It's summer and
the children are out playing."

Months later, Abby wakes her father, Anthony, a big highway plow. She asks the same question.

"Almost, but not yet," her father replies. "The leaves are many colors and they are falling. Winter is coming soon."

More months go by and a few snowflakes appear. The Plow family is up and ready, except for Abby. She's still sleeping.

Now the snow is really falling and
settles on the ground. "Wake up, Abby,"
says Mommy Plow. "Winter is here!"

On the other side of town, Maya stares out her window. She is sad and doesn't want it to snow.

She turns to her parents, holding her holiday play costume. "I want there to be school today. We worked so hard for our school play."

Her parents smile and point out the window. "Here come the Plows!"

Down the snow-filled street come the Plows.

As the Plows come closer to the house,
a school bus appears behind them.

Abby happily plows a path up the
driveway. Maya waits at the door
to greet the little Plow.

"Thank you," Maya says to Abby as she pats Abby's hood. The school bus has pulled up and waits for Maya.

Maya boards the
school bus as the Plows
join together and smile.

As the Plow family drives away
together, Abby smiles and says,
"Winter is my favorite time of year!"

Jamie and Chuck Freedman live with their two sons in a small New England town north of Boston. Chuck loves the snow, while Jamie would prefer not to live in an area that gets 3 times the national average snow fall. Although Chuck has been published as a technical writer, *Welcome To Plow Town* is their first children's book and first creative collaboration together -- not counting their amazing sons, of course.

Founded in 2010, Red Seat Media, LLC is a creative production company with a vision to produce all kinds of enriching media and entertainment.

Visit redseatmedia.com or follow @RedSeatMedia on Twitter to learn of the company's new projects, upcoming releases and ideas.

Visit plowtown.com and follow @PlowTown on Twitter to learn about news, new books, games, new digital releases of *Welcome to Plow Town* and to order copies of this book for anyone you know who would love it.

Kory Fluckiger is a fine artist and illustrator based in Salt Lake City, UT. His paintings and illustrations can be seen on his website at: www.koryfluckiger.com

Have a book idea?

Contact us at:

Mascot Books

560 Herndon Parkway

Suite 120

Herndon, VA

info@mascotbooks.com | www.mascotbooks.com

The authors of this book
recommend these books, also
available from Mascot Books:

A Place to Get Well

Alfred the Alligator Visits Mount Vernon

Countdown 'til Daddy Comes Home

Elephant on Deck

Pumpkin the Therapy Dog

So Big Yet So Small

Wally the Green Monster and His World Tour

Wally the Green Monster's Journey Through Time

and, of course,

Doing a Great Job, by Jamie and Chuck Freedman